Of Monsters that Sift Our Blood

Of Monsters that Sift Our Blood

B.A.D.

As in order of…

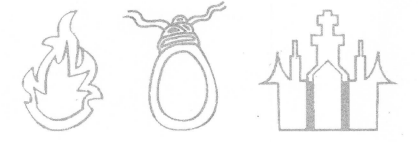

A Rare Crossing with Cornelius Hunter

"Beware the man... *Cornelius Hunter*" whispered the angels.

"Heed all courses away from that particular soul" advised the devils.

"Flee, scurry, retreat, and hide" warned the beasts.

"An anomaly" rumored the gods, "What mortal could have ever become such a being? Surely the universe must have forgotten of him in Its making... and now we, who follow the rules and are bound to Its laws, must fear this... *monster.*"

"Cornelius Hunter, and his dreadful hounds" contemplated the invisible spectators, "What rite, what trial, what initiation or ritual was it that granted him such power? We watched and saw nothing strange nor anything that led to this development.

... It would seem that he always had this power, but such was not the case for it would've been sensed far earlier. Born without it, but was sure to obtain it; sure to obtain it, for he was born with it— a paradox like the universe itself.

Why does it feel like we— the judgers —are now in setting to be judged?

Fare, all we can do now is ensure we do not cross his path..."

Vera had been lost now for hours, wondering blindly through this ghostly landscape which seemed to want nothing more than to scare her.

There was an endless fog that never lifted, and although at times it would thin-out to near vanishment... the opposite was equally as true, and it would thicken densely into a shroud heavier than that of night.

A strange hue of green encapsulated everything in this world as if the sun bore a light shun through an emerald, yet oddly enough... no sun could be found when one looked up into the sky.

The ground had the most gentle vibration to it which seemed to hum beneath the earth. It wasn't intrusive nor obnoxious, but subtle and almost secretive— noticed only when one stood stationary and if their mind had peace to notice it.

But a peaceful mind was no luxury to be found in this place, as Vera was constantly harassed and haunted by its environment.

When everything seemed still, faded echoes from some distant wails could be heard.

When everything felt hectic during her stumbles through these fogged woods, the sensation of being vulnerable at every angle and every moment gnawed at her bones.

With no sense of direction, no knowledge of where she was, no awareness of what might be lurking within these woods or behind the cloak of thick fog surrounding her, Vera trekked around this landscape aimlessly—

using only the unsettling sounds of twigs snapping, beasts yawning, wails groaning, and creatures chittering as her guide for something to move away from… for surely safety must have lied in opposition to these freakish sounds.

This strategy of hers had been successful in terms of avoiding those hidden horrors that existed all around her, but bore no real fruit in the grand escape from whatever these cursed woods were and wherever this nightmare of a world was.

However… that all changed when the dog-like howls sung their tune.

The howls themselves did not sound nefarious or malicious in any way, in fact, they sounded quite beautiful and harmonious as they were in sync with each other from whatever pack roamed in formation— producing a silky and mystique ringing akin to something achieved by an a-cappella with melodious intent.

But it was by the way which these woods and the creatures within them responded to these howls that set an ominous tone.

Like the silencing of crickets when danger is near, or the quieting of cicadas when a predator appears, the lost woods went absolutely dead upon the echoes of those howls. Even the atmosphere felt subject to those beasts' harmonic call, for the hum of the ground ceased and the fog swiftly dissipated as though it had been pierced at its core.

And with the clearing of that great fog, and the cease of motion in the world around her, Vera finally had a moment to look around and observe where she was and what lay in her vicinity.

… But there was nothing.

Just trees and dirt and leaves and air...

It was as though everything that had once resided within the fog had also left with it upon the hearing of those howls.

Vera was all alone, which felt worse than when she was surrounded by those unknown horrors just moments ago— for now she was the oddball out. Before, she was an equal to the terror and the disturbed that lived in what she could describe as a harmony of an ecosystem based in all that is dread and danger. It was all equal, it was all fair ground... even if she was at the bottom of that food chain.

But this recognition by everything within the woods that those mysterious howls were connected to something far greater, far more powerful, something beyond any and all power that once prowled within the fog, or roamed amongst the green skies, or slithered atop the vibrating earth... there was no equal standing here— hence their flee.

And so, Vera was left as the oddball. Not because she was the weakest, but because she did not have the awareness to flee at first sound of those howls, nor did she have the ability to disappear so quickly with the fog.

Then suddenly, from behind her, the sounds of hollow cracks and pops could be heard shifting around in fluid motion— like an old man stretching his appendages while the air between his joints collapsed.

Vera didn't even have a moment to turn around or a second to run away before those hollow sounds were followed by a physical force, as she was snatched from behind and squeezed out of breath by the being that stood behind her!

"The hunt has begun!" warned the thing that took hold of her.

Face to face with her captor, Vera could now observe the nightmare who spoke, as looming over her now with a tight clutch around her body was a waking tree.

Two of its largest branches had turned into arms which fully wrapped around her torso, creating an inescapable hold.

A giant face emerged out of the trunk, rough and sculpted of bark, with eyes sunken in by pits where animals would make nest.

"An abomination draws near..." continued the waking tree, *"May we innocent souls not stir any interest in his gaze, nor let his devious grip catch hold of our essence— we pray!"*

The waking tree pulled Vera in closer, *"You must run, child. Upon all things that exist in the worlds, do not let* **he** *be your end, for there is no more after that... the maniacal Monster!*

His hounds are about and they seek their prey. Whatever wretched creature it is that has culled forth his wrath has now sought refuge here— in our world —damning us all until its capture is celebrated or its flee takes to yet another world."

Rabid barking began to fill the air, and its volume only increased as the hounds producing them drew closer in proximity.

"Go now!" strained the waking tree, releasing Vera from its grip and shoving her away towards the ground, *"May you find escape from this monster's approach.*

Allow the deranged creatures of these woods to rip out your throat or tear open your heart— any death but by him will keep you safe."

The face on the tree slowly began to sink back into the trunk, and the bark smoothed over the defining details as it returned to being an inconspicuous shape of a normal tree. As the arms lifted and hardened back into their normal structure of two average branches, a final whisper could be heard from the waking tree now slumbered, *"Run... for you lack the blessing of hiding."*

Vera wished she had more time to process the whole event of everything that had just occurred: from her arrival into these strange and foreign lands different from her original world; to the sounds of the creatures that had previously shared her company in the fog; to the tree that just held her dearly and spoke to her; to this warning of the deadly man and his wicked hounds now.

However, she did not have the time to sit with any of it, for that last bit of information which presented itself to her was the very reason why she had to run and not look back.

And so, Vera broke into a sprint, her feet stomping against the brittle earth with clumps breaking and dispersing in her wake.

Her lungs ached more than her legs burned from the tremendous toll she put on them, but she dared not to stop for a moment as the ravenous howls and salivated yaps with anxious whines only grew closer on her tail.

However... her fleeing efforts were met in vain.

Vera couldn't tell you if it was a tree root she had tripped over, or her own two feet, or a hole in the ground, or if her legs had just given out as a form of surrendering to the inevitable... but the reason did not matter and the conclusion remained the same— slamming chest first into the ground, so hard in fact that it bumped her up again like a rock skipping across water, Vera took a tumble with steep momentum, sending her flying and colliding against a tree.

Dazed, confused, and body throbbing between intervals of acute pain and buzzing numbness, she brought all her limbs in closely to her body and tucked her head away between her arms and legs like any scared child does.

Her threshold for fear had finally been reached, and although death itself was a terrifying idea, it was the thought and visual of it happening that truly broke her spirit.

So she squeezed her eyes shut as hard as she could and then braced for the worst.

Barks turned to growls, and the pattering of beasts' feet could be heard surrounding her.

While all the others stayed in their circled position, the deep rumble from one hungry growl grew closer— shortly followed by the sensation of its breath huffing hotly onto Vera's legs, arms, and head as it sniffed her out.

Anxiety and anticipation made this short moment feel stretched out, as all Vera could do was wonder when this monstrous beast was going to sink its teeth into her flesh, and which part of her body would it start on.

However, all of that immense fear, dread, and panic felt washed away in an instant… when the mysterious beast gave a single lick across her arm.

Still timid and moving very slowly with extreme caution, Vera lifted her head from her bodily shield and opened her eyes to a limited squint.

Circled before her now were four bloodhounds— almost normal looking ones too, as their appearance did not unsettle her soul or bring back the previous fear she had so quickly let go of.

But by no means did they look completely average.

These ones were far, **far** larger, standing taller and broader as if doubled in size for its breed.

Their eyes were of a golden color and bright— not glowing independently by their own nature, but shimmering magnificently against the light that already existed around them.

And their saliva was not gooey nor dripping— but ethereal and weightless, rising up from their jowls in a swirling dance like beautiful smoke.

The attention of all four of these giant hounds remained completely on Vera, but their growls, howls, and barking had fully ceased. In fact, all the vicious intent that was previously sensed by their distant presence had now changed since that single lick.

It might have been because of how great and unique these dogs were, or maybe from the fact that they were the cause for her previous moments of terror, that Vera hadn't noticed the man standing feet behind them until he spoke.

"Girl" said a grizzly and bold voice. It was authoritative by nature and intimidating from the strength held behind it... but also reassuring and simultaneously curious from the softness in its ending tone.

Vera's eyes darted up from the hound in front of her to the man standing behind it.

She was startled by his presence, and instinctively took in all his details in an observation of survival.

He was neither remarkably tall nor remarkably short. The only thing that stood out about his body was the way he was dressed, donning a long and weathered coat which looked to be made of leather by the dark water stains, rippled creases, and numerous scratches of lighter color.

On his head sat a hat, bent and misshaped— like a worn out cowboy's but more befitting of a hunter.

And his boots were covered in dirt and dried mud, the caked up parts broken off by his continual adventure as opposed to a mindful cleaning or upkeep.

"You're worlds away from your own" said the man as he approached Vera until he stood directly before her, "What are you doing in these lands? This is not the place for a human, let alone a child."

No different than how a dog or cat hides its belly in a misconceived notion of protecting their vulnerability, Vera hid her voice in similar fashion— feeling as if her safety was at greater risk by speaking.

So without uttering a single word, Vera shook her head in response, informing the mysterious man of both her lack of knowledge to how she ended up in this green lit realm, as well as to her "on guard" nature.

The man took a deep breath in through his nostrils and sighed it out his mouth, "Well, no matter the case, it is not safe for you here.

Come. We will find shelter."

As if they were aware of the statement that the man had just made and carried the ability to understand language, the hounds immediately bounded past the tree Vera laid against— this time without their barks or growls.

When the hound that had licked Vera out of her fearful state also continued on its way forward, Vera quickly turned around past the tree to watch it leave— a reflex of holding onto the object that carried her sensation of safety.

That specific hound only made it a handful of feet away before it stopped in its tracks, and the man spoke again, "Does that one bring you comfort?" he asked.

Vera looked at the man and gave him a desperate nod.

"Very well."

And just like before, the hound responded in an instant and turned around, making its way back to the two of them and placing its body right beside Vera.

"Go ahead" continued the man, "Pick yourself up. Let's not waste anymore time sitting in fear. Let it dissipate slowly as we walk."

Following the man's instructions, Vera reached her arms onto the hound's back and pulled herself up from the ground.

The man began to walk and the hound followed suit beside him, so Vera followed them as well— keeping close to the animal with a hand never leaving its back as to maintain that sensation of security it provided her.

They walked in silence for a large portion of the time, long enough for Vera to finally feel safe again despite the madness she had recently endured and start to feel comfortable... or rather, familiarity by the man and his hound's presence.

It was only by the retreating of terror that once consumed her that Vera realized this mysterious man was the only other normal person she had encountered in this ominous world, and his hounds were the closest thing to a normal animal that she'd seen or heard in hours.

"What's its name?" asked Vera, regaining her voice and confidence.

"It doesn't have one" responded the mysterious man, keeping his focus forward and towards wherever they were heading.

"Why doesn't it have a name?" inquired Vera.

"Because that would not make sense."

There was an awkward pause, one which was created by Vera not wanting to get in trouble by asking more questions like any innocent child would feel, and therefore, she held her tongue while still drenched in confusion and a loss for true understanding.

The man must have sensed this though, because he broke that silence by following up his previous statement with, "Does your hand have a name? Your left one or your right? Do the fingers on that hand have a name?"

Vera shook her head.

"No" agreed the man, "Because they are *your* hands, *your* fingers. They **are** you— there is no separation."

"What's your name, then?" asked Vera.

"Cornelius. Cornelius Hunter.

And you, girl?"

"I'm Vera."

"Vera…" repeated Cornelius, "What's the age and year of where you come from?" he asked.

"The Blackened Age of Iron and Magic, 300 years post claiming" she responded.

"Hm" grunted Cornelius, the information meaning more to him with wherever his mind was currently roaming with it.

"Where are we going?" asked Vera.

"To shelter" answered Cornelius, "There is a shack further ahead. We'll camp there for the night. And tomorrow, after I finish my business here, I'll take you home. Back to your own world where you belong."

Vera couldn't help but think that Cornelius— in all of his quiet manner, and despite the dangerous air that loomed over him and his hounds —seemed nice.

"Before you found me, a tree had grabbed me and warned that a monster was approaching… a monster and his hounds" said Vera.

Cornelius' gaze and stride did not falter by Vera's pry, and he seemed completely unfazed by the accusation being questioned by the young child.

"I think the tree was referring to you— or rather, I thought."

"Do you think I'm a monster?" asked Cornelius.

"No. But you are scary" admitted Vera.

"Are all scary things monsters, then? If so, then it's true what the humans say when they preach *we create our own monsters*'.

Tell me, do you find a spider the size of your fingernail that has snuck onto your pillow a monster?"

Vera shook her head.

"But I'm certain the tiny creature scared you. But it is no monster.

How about a giant beast like a lion that can maul you to death in a second? Do you think a lion is a monster?"

Vera shook her head again.

"No, of course not. Scary, yes— but even though a lion's more capable of killing you than a spider, it is still no monster."

Vera drifted into her own thoughts as she pondered what Cornelius had just proposed to her.

She had never considered this perspective, and now it danced within her mind.

Once again, Cornelius was able to pick up on these thoughts that consumed the girl, and gave a helping hand to these festering thoughts.

"Two things are responsible for the common conception or assumption of a monster: one belonging to the mind, and one belonging to the soul.

The first one is created by a grotesque appearance or a fearful idea— a response from the mind caused by a present visual or by a thought looking outwards towards the future.

The second one is created by an evil aura— a response from the soul picking up on a nefarious energy.

It only takes one of those two things to make you think you're facing down a monster, and both of them for you to believe it.

You'll probably see a lot of scary things during your life, Vera. Probably already have since you somehow ended up in this world far from home. And now... it's inevitable that you will only continue to be exposed to the hidden horrors of life that most humans live in a luxury blind to.

Hopefully you never encounter a real monster, and avoid such beings at all cost.

However, if they do impose onto your life regardless of your efforts, and cross into your peace..." Cornelius stopped his march for the first time and looked down at Vera to meet her eyes with his own, "Kill it" he said sternly, "Permanently. Then return to your peace, and continue avoiding such monsters."

In that moment, Vera felt the most overwhelming, endless surging, pungent and all-consuming dread which she had never experienced in her life before. It made her more than scared— it made her hopeless, nauseas, and heavy as if gravity became ten times stronger.

This must have been what the other creatures of these woods felt when they scurried from the sound of the hounds' howls. This must have been the reason for the waking tree's warning of the man.

For the way Cornelius spoke those words now so casually yet confident... and the way they held an undeniable absoluteness within them... this sensation— this power that he held —this was the thing that nightmares could only attempt to mimic... to feel like. It was the thing that gods falsely portrayed themselves as having, and hoped to be perceived as carrying.

And in repeated pattern, Cornelius knew just how Vera felt in this moment and what she was thinking, which caused him to re-engage once again to allay the current mood.

He lifted his arm and pointed ahead of them, "The shack's just ahead. Come.

It has a fireplace. A fire sounds nice right about now."

The idea of a fire was such a simple thing, and yet it provided a familiar reassurance which wiped away all of the dread that was drowning Vera mere seconds ago.

Along with that, a new curiosity had caught her attention— Cornelius' hand.

When he pointed ahead, she noticed that his finger looked odd. It was short, as if it were missing a digit...

Without dwelling on it for too long, Vera followed Cornelius and his hound a couple more yards, where the three of them soon found themselves crossing out of the woods and into a small clearing of land.

At the center of this clearing was a small shack made of wood, with darkened planks fortifying its exterior and a boarded up window hanging beside the door... a door which was already open as the three other hounds stood guard beside it.

"Is there anyone inside?" asked Vera as they made their way closer.

"No" answered Cornelius, "I've already scouted the place. There's no one and no *thing* within it or nearby. It's safe to spend the night here. Do not fret."

Once the two entered, Vera noted the simplicity of the shack's interior, consisting of a small bed sat along the furthest corner of the wall, an even smaller table with two chairs sat by the planked up window, and a robust looking fireplace made of a cylindrical piece of blackened iron, filled with ash from its forgotten use long ago, bearing a connecting piece of pipe that stretched upward and out onto the roof to expel any smoke.

Though this shack was barren and left dead by even the spiders who had long abandoned their webs within… it still carried a certain amount of comfort and warmth— a coziness both belonging to and only offered to the humans who might have once roamed this strange green realm.

"I will make us a fire" said Cornelius as he stepped outside of the shack, "You may have the bed for the night— I have no requirement for sleep"

Vera watched from the inside as he ripped off the planks of wood that boarded the window and brought them back inside. He then snapped them in half, dividing their size and doubling their numbers, before tossing them into the fireplace.

Though it seemed logical to think that nothing should be able to spook or surprise Vera at this point after having witnessed the waking tree, the giant hounds with their glowing eyes, hearing the roars of the creatures in the mist, or the pure fact that she was in a different world all together from her own… it still came as a shock to her comprehension when the wood spontaneously combusted into flames after Cornelius finished placing it all into the fireplace.

But the thing that stood out the most— what made it most astonishing — was how he didn't do anything to start it.

There was no whisper enchanted, or spell spoken. No wave of the hand, or snap of the fingers. Not a squint of the eyes, nor a huff of the breath.

There was absolutely nothing that showed his effort or power in conjuring the fire. And yet, it was undoubtedly him who caused those flames to erupt, as it coincided in perfect synchronicity with his finishing of preparing the wood.

"How did you do that?" asked Vera, curious and fascinated.

"The fire?" he clarified as he took a seat at the little table.

Vera nodded.

"I made fire" answered Cornelius, "Simple as that."

"My mother told me tales of witches" began Vera, taking the other seat at the table, "She said they could control all sorts of things with magick. Animals, people, fate, shadows, and even the elements— like fire.

And my dad told me tales of gods. He said some of them rule over certain things or certain forces, and therefore, can control them and manipulate them.

Things like the ocean. Things like love. Things like fire.

But in my mother's tales of witches, they had to use spells. They had to say the right words or do the right proceedings first.

And in my father's tales of gods, they had to channel it. They had to at least lift their arm to make it rise, or close their fist to snuff it away.

So how did you make the fire… if you did neither?"

"Ah. You're very observant. And very smart for your age, too" commented Cornelius, "Your mother and father did you well to teach you of such things at a young age, and you've done even better by putting that knowledge into use like you did just now.

But that makes me very suspicious of how a girl with such wisdom and intuition managed to get misplaced in a realm like this.

So tell you what... I'll answer your question— though be warned, it's a rather long one as these things require explaining. And upon the explaining, you'll be introduced to new concepts, truths, and theories which will require even more explaining.

But... in return, you must tell me how you arrived here.

Deal?"

Vera nervously shuffled in her seat, but nodded and agreed, "Deal."

For the first time since they met, Cornelius smiled. It was a wicked yet warm grin— not necessarily threatening, but certainly one with an indomitable power behind it.

"You're an intelligent child, and I believe you have the capacity to comprehend and keep up with what I say, so I will not stupefy my words.

Let us start by challenging what you know as 'reality', and what better place to start than with the very examples you gave me— the witch and the gods.

Now, it is true as you said: witches can manipulate the fire, and so can the gods.

So tell me this, Vera, if a witch who has mastered the arts of fire was to battle a god who held domain over the element... who would win?"

"The god" answered Vera.

"And why do you think that?"

"Because the god is a more powerful being" responded Vera, "The witch *uses* power to manipulate the fire. The god *is* that power of fire. It's why witches pray to gods, or demons, or entities— to gain further assistance and ability in understanding such powers so they can better grasp and wield them."

"Hmph. I can see your mother knows much about the craft" said Cornelius, "But let's see if your father knows much about the gods.

So, Vera, if the gods— or more specifically, a god of fire, or one who holds some domain over it, *is* the power of fire, meaning they are akin to it; at one with it; unified, harmonized, and a part of it... then how come ordinary man can summon it so?

That's the equivalent of having the power to summon a god, is it not?

And contrary to the faithful, summoning a god or any being for that matter is no simple feat.

Your father must have taught you that.

In fact, witches know that better than any to be true, as they are the most capable and likely to actually summon such beings and do it successfully. Something I'm sure your mother has mentioned."

"Well because fire doesn't belong to either the god or the witch. They both just have the power to control and manipulate it— a power that comes from a deep understanding of fire."

"Correct!" exclaimed Cornelius, "Fire is its own force. Its own power. Something that stands alone... on its own. But it is still able to be experienced in whatever varying degree it can be by all beings, by all life, by all matter and types of essences across the infinite universes.

And just like how love, or death, or chaos is merely an aspect of the universe— something already woven into the fabric of its structure —so too is fire.

Fire is an element. It is part of a structure that already exists, a structure woven into the very structure of our reality— not since the beginning because there was no beginning... but rather, it just always was.

Therefore, those things such as love, death, chaos, fire, water, air, earth, and so forth— which have gods' names attached to them— does not mean that those gods created those things... because they did not. Those things always existed far before those beings did.

So if the god is not that power, then they are no different than the witch. And the witch is no different than the ordinary man. The only thing that separates them all from each other is how they are able to manipulate the fire.

Ordinary man controls the fire by a system of organic law— wood, oil, tinder, friction, sparks —man did not create the fire, those other things did. Those things create the fire because reactions are a fundamental gear to the machine of reality.

The witch controls the fire by a means of power— spells, magick, the craft, the dark arts, the esoteric ways, the forgotten truths or the hidden secrets —these things are tools, and these tools are very special because they allow you to interact, traverse, manipulate and shape the universe in a very special way. Fire already exists, whether it's in front of you now or not— it exists in the universe for it is a structure of it. Unlike ordinary man who uses a reaction to create a fire within their space, a witch merely conjures the fire and brings it forth to them. They needn't a reaction to create it, for like I said, fire already exists and is a structure of the universe— so instead, they use the tools of magick to interact with the universe in a unique way and bring forth fire through conjuration. *'That which exists... now exists here!'* And to be honest, that is just as much natural as the system of organic law, though it's not as widely understood and known.

Now the god, the god controls the fire because they have a very deep, unique, and intimate relationship with the element— similar character, shared principles, a bleeding heart for one another —like any deep relationship, it comes from an even deeper understanding of the other. You needn't ask your partner to kiss you, or hold your hand, or tell you they love you— you need only lean in close, or extend your hand, or give them a smile, and from these tiny and incomplete gestures alone they will answer you back with what you desire... because they know exactly what you're asking for and what you desire by those gestures. And the thing is, they want to do those things for you equally as much as you desire them. When you are in a relationship with someone, or in this case, *something*, you are not separate from it— you are no longer just simply you, nor are you *'me and them'*, or *'they and I'*. You are now *'us'*, you are now *'we'*, you are now... a *couple*. It becomes a singular reference to the pair because they are bonded, they come with each other."

"But what about fire itself?" asked Vera, "If the element itself was to manifest into a sentient form?

That would be the **true** god of fire, wouldn't it? The fire, which was never created but always existed, was to create a form or version of itself that stood alone while simultaneously encompassing its own element?"

Cornelius huffed in amusement, "My theory about you was correct. You *are* more than just a lost girl in a realm you don't belong in. We'll address that later, though I already have certain suspicions. However, we'll keep to the conversation at play.

To answer your question: Yes.

Fire itself manifested into a sentient form would be the true god of fire. Truer than any god who may hold a domain in it. And certainly truer than any witch or man who wields a fraction of it.

However, you must understand that even if fire manifested into a sentient form of itself… all other fire would **not** disappear.

The non sentient version— the pure elemental state that is woven into the fabric of the universe, which man, witch and god all call upon —would still exist. And the random fires that occur in nature by organic law and from the different reactions rooted in weather, space, chemistry, and circumstances would all still play out in their own accord.

Sure, the now sentient form of fire would have rule over these occurrings when faced with them, or presented to them, or made aware of them. But the mere fact that it is now a sentient form *means* that it is no longer all of those fires in all of those places all at once. *That* is the critical truth which every man, witch, and god always looks over in such a thing.

If fire manifests into a sentient form— when **anything** becomes sentient… that merely means it's become self-aware. And self-awareness is the first part— the *first step* —in no longer being a *piece* of the universe's structure, but now instead an *experiencer* of the universe's structure. It is independence. It is individualism.

That is what consciousness is, girl.

Consciousness makes you an experiencer. Consciousness makes you an individual. You are now a sovereign being— no matter what your thoughts may have once or continue to still encompass.

That means that that god of fire, who is fire itself manifested into a sentient form... is in fact, now separate from fire. And although it may be the closest thing to the original element compared to any other being that holds domain over the element, the truth is... any fire that that sentient form now creates is its *own* fire; any fire that it encounters outside of itself which it then chooses to manipulate or change is actually not connected to it, but rather, just very close to it. Close to it like a memory, or the nostalgia of an old home which you've grown out of— not something to return to, but something you know very well and hold dearly, but are no longer a part of.

Do you understand?"

Vera nodded, "I think so."

"Good. Well then, there you have it" said Cornelius, "The long version to answer your question. A version that will also aid in the next question which you were bound to ask me sooner or later.

So tell me, do you now know how I made the fire?"

Vera frowned, "You did not create the fire in the same sense by which a witch or god or man would. You created the fire in the same sense that a sentient god of fire itself would... which means it was not *the* fire, or *a* fire, it was *your* fire— sovereign and separate from the mechanics of the universe and even the element itself... for it was yours. It was you."

"Correct. Now, for the next question which you were bound to ask. Because you never asked it earlier, but only referred to it. And I never answered it, only deferred from it…"

"Are you a monster?" asked Vera, "For a moment, after your long explanation, I was going to ask if you were in fact, a sentient form of fire manifested. But then I realized all of that was a reference for me to better understand… meaning you are different from all those examples… something more. Those examples were for me to gain the ability to better understand whatever you are."

"I am a monster" answered Cornelius bluntly, "The truest form of a monster that can exist, because everything would consider me one. The gods, the angels, the demons, the beasts, the good, the evil, the neutral… all of them unanimously consider me a monster.

And I agree. I understand. Compared to them and everything else in the all of existence and the spiraling continuation of the universe… how could I not be?"

"But what makes you a monster? What is it about you that would make all those beings across their vast differences agree on that single fact about you?"

"Because I am no longer a part of the game" answered Cornelius, "I am sovereign from even the universe itself, now. I am truly, wholly, and only… me."

"… I don't understand" responded Vera after a long pause.

"That's okay" reassured Cornelius, "It's not an easy concept, so I expected as much. But allow me to make this understanding flow for you. Let us reference back to the idea of fire manifested into a sentient version of itself.

And for that, I'd like to ask you something.

Your father, he taught you about the gods, so surely he taught you about religions then, yes?"

Vera nodded.

"Did he teach you of the religions whose goal is to return to being at one with the universe? Returning to source, being blended back into the fabric of reality, perfectly merged with the essence of the all— the all that is… with everything?"

Vera nodded again.

"Good" continued Cornelius, "Now, let's look at that in reference to the fire that manifested sentience.

It's a god of fire yet separate from fire itself now. So, to return to its original source, to return to fire and be a part of it, no longer separate from it as a whole, then that would mean abandoning its sentience.

And by abandoning its sentience and returning to being a part of fire— fire the element —it is then returning to being a part of the universe itself, as fire is just an aspect of the universe.

But you see, Vera, that's not just a circumstance for the fire that became sentient… it's the circumstance for everyone one of you" said Cornelius pointing at her with his missing digit finger, "And every creature out there" he said pointing out the window, "Every god. Every man. Every witch, demon, angel, mortal, immortal, and every other being that has sentience.

For that is what the universe is. It is simultaneously repeating as it is expanding. More is infinitely being added as it grows bigger, and more is infinitely becoming new as it expands further.

And all those new things and all those new additions become folded back into the universe and its reality, then merged with the things that already exist, and experienced alongside with all that was... and with all that is now.

This repeating cycle of being at one with it all, growing a sentience, self-awareness, a consciousness, to then becoming the experiencer of it all, and with that, growing ourselves, until eventually we reach a point where we rejoin being with all of everything as it continues to grow and expand... until we, now both a part of and an aspect of the universe, grow sentience once again, then get to experience the universe ourselves, grow from such experiences, return, and so forth and so on... constant new additions, constant expansion, constant growth, forever and ever.

You see, the symbol for the universe is a spiral. But what most don't know is that it is not spiraling inwards... it is spiraling outwards in this pattern of repeated expansion."

"And that spiral" said Vera, slowly piecing it together as she spoke, "You are no longer a part of it? No longer a part of the universe?"

"Precisely" answered Cornelius casually, "And that spiral, although it expands outward and is ever growing with constant new additions... it still looked more like a prison to me. Might as well have been spiraling inwards from my perspective."

"But why would that make you a monster?" asked Vera, "It just sounds like another path, perhaps a rarer one... but not a terrible thing of monsters."

"Because by not being a part of the universe, I am outside of its rules. I am not bound to any of its divine laws or unbreakable structures.

And you simplify it too much, Vera. It's not just a rare path... it's the unnamed one. It's a state of being.

Most return to source and become one with the universe at some point, and then eventually attain sentience again, repeating that process over and over again. But some reach a point in power— sovereignty of the mind, body and soul —where they choose not to return to being at one with the universe, however they are still very much a part of the universes structure and flow.

To break off from it all, to truly stand on your own... that's the few. Less than the few, in fact."

"But what's the difference then between the beings who choose to not return to source but instead remain in their sentience, and you?" asked Vera, seeking more clarification.

"The difference is that they are still bound to its divine laws. Still attached to its sacred rules. Still a part of its complex structure.

And why wouldn't they wanna be? It's not a bad thing to be a part of it all, not by any means.

Truly, it's a guarantee— the best one you can ask for. For there is no end. It's all eternal.

And it's ever growing. Ever expanding. New blossoms growing every instant for eternity in a never ending infinity for you to experience.

You're too young right now for good reference, but when you grow older, you will understand this and better appreciate it: you have eternal opportunity to do better; to be better; to grow more; to experience more; to understand deeper; to become that which you truly are and even more. Be it in this life or the next. This sentience or the next" Cornelius sighed, "... It is not an easy thing to break away from.

For if you do, the universe will no longer be the unknown and invisible guiding hand in your life that helps and pushes you in the unseen ways for your benefit.

There is no more fate for you to fall on, or destiny to catch you.

You are truly separated from it all, and therefore, utterly all alone.

But that's why the divine laws and the sacred structures cannot touch or rule me in any way."

"... Why would you want to separate yourself from the universe if you describe it in such a positive way?" asked Vera.

"Personal preference" answered Cornelius, "And personal perspective.

Most beings view that cycle as *'One will always return to source'*. However, I view it as *'One will always return to sentience'*.

And the thing is, the beings that choose to stay in their sentience almost always begin *the game*. It becomes this play of power— a disgusting snow-ball of understanding the universe and its structure the most as opposed to experiencing it.

So on the one hand you have these ancient beings who have chosen to stay in their sentience and have now begun to play the game— it's no longer about experiencing, its all about power, and the moment you start achieving real levels of sentience again… you're likely to find yourself being orchestrated by them, or at the very least, pushing heads against them to not be.

And on the other hand you have the option of returning to source, returning to being all, where it's pure bliss as you're merely experiencing yourself and the everything of all, all at once, in its beautiful flow and expansion.

But the issue with the latter is that at some point… you *will* regain sentience again, and achieve sovereign individuality again from the source of all. And when that happens, you will get to grow and experience for a short while before achieving real levels of sentience once more, then being thrown right back into the game and fighting against the orchestration of the beings who remained sentient.

So… if you're always going to return to that, and you don't like that… then how do you make the change?

Within mortal structures, we can easily see corruption. And within immortal structures and the structures of the universe, it would seem that we can see and say the same thing.

Tired, exhausted, and hopeless, I saw the flaw in these ancient beings' ways, as well as the universe for that matter— its structure and divine laws and failure in allowing such things to go on.

… And then… like the awakening process of coming into awareness itself, I recognized the exact fundamental flaw of the game, and how it sucks in even those who do not wish to be a part of it— even those who despise it.

The game is understanding the universe the most. Understanding its structure the best. Understanding its aspects the deepest. All so you can just manipulate it the most, for that is the power within knowing these things. And these ancient beings who held onto their sentience seek it, for that is what they believe is the purpose in eternal sentience. And for all those who disagree and wish merely to experience the universe in their eternal sentience... well, now they too fall into the game as they seek to gain the most understanding of the universe just so that they can be outside of these ancient being's touch, and their ugly orchestrations.

The orchestrations only happen because it speeds up their ploys set in place, which have been created by them to further gain deeper understandings in a more speedy and efficient way. Think like this, you can learn a lesson and gain its teachings just by observing and finding out the realizations that another being came to understand from an experience, no different than you can from having experienced it and going through it yourself. So imagine how much clarity you can achieve from organizing multiple lives outside of your own to experience certain lessons through different obstacles in life while you get to bear witness to their numerous insights all at once, as opposed to living and enduring those lessons yourself through just one singular experience at a time that could take upwards of a whole lifetime, or multiple lifetimes of strenuous mental, spiritual, emotional, and physical toll.

Now the thing is, those who seek to gain power and understandings purely to be outside of these despicable beings touch and to not be used in their selfish turmoil... will eventually take part in doing the same.

It starts out small and minor, of course— no where near on the same scale, and no where near the same violation of free will —but it is still an orchestration, nonetheless.

Do you see how the game sucks in even the beings that don't want to participate in it? Its fuel being the mere fact that they wish to not be a part of it?" Cornelius shook his head, "These stupid, selfish, and sloppy beings inadvertently created the inward spiral of the universe, when it should be outward."

Cornelius leaned in close to Vera, his tone and face direly serious, "A terrible ignorance has spread itself across the cosmos and the fabric of the universe like a parasite.

And the secret to immunity from this ignorance, this parasitic and make-shift dogma of repulsive inversion from the truth— the secret to escaping it all, is merely the original purpose and intention of existence that always was and always meant to be… to come into absolute union with yourself, and to hold the greatest understanding of **yourself** above anything else.

There is no need to understand every thread of each fiber that makes up the universe, or every intricate line of the divine law, or every essence of the infinite multitudes which exist and are constantly being birthed into reality.

That's not where true power comes from nor will it ever be. That is a never ending game of consumption in a repulsive attempt to finally stand above it all at the top of everything— believing you have finally succeeded in the journey of life and achieved that view from the peak of the cosmic mountain because you have accomplished the greatest feat in existence that consciousness is meant to achieve… but that's wrong.

… That's an ouroboros… infinitely eating its own tail.

You see, Vera, you never needed to know any of that. I'm not saying that you won't ever come across such knowledge, nor that you should avoid it. However, I am saying that it should never be your focus. For it will never make a difference.

You do not need to know how molecules and atoms make up your body's physical form and how they work— only that this is *your* body, and the harmony of being completely at one with it.

You needn't understand exactly how your intention and your soul and your heart are able to accelerate any magick you cast as a witch— only that you are the carrier of your own intention, the bearer of your own soul, the beholder of your own heart. You are all those things at once, therefore, you need only be in tune with them, and understand them, to be aware of the simple fact that you *are* those things, and to be at one with this awareness along with all the feelings they produce.

As I said before, the universe is ever growing and ever expanding. But look at the direction it is growing and expanding in— compare the pursuits of the ignorant and selfish beings I spoke of earlier, to the recommendations I gave you just now. This universe and its expansion sounds a lot more like chaos to me... when it should be *love*.

So where is the love in all of that madness? The stable kind of love? The one that is grounded, unshakable, can never be uprooted and is eternal despite any circumstance or condition?" Cornelius slowly pointed at Vera, "It's right there. *It's you.*

Because you know yourself absolutely. You are in tune with yourself completely. You are harmonized with your entire being. So it doesn't matter what aspect of the universe you are faced with, or what new truths come your way, or what new condition enters your space, or what new addition has been birthed into existence... for it will always be *you* facing it, *you* amongst it, *you* experiencing it.

And even the changes that occur within you— the changes that you go through because you too are ever growing and ever expanding —will remain grounded as a certainty amongst the chaos of uncertainty… for it is *you* going through those changes."

Vera frowned, "But that doesn't sound special. That doesn't sound like a secret. That sounds like the obvious, like all roads and crossroads would eventually lead to such an understanding that pushes towards the pursuit of investing in the self. "

Cornelius smiled as if relieved by Vera's words, "It brings me great comfort and hope to hear that you feel that way, Vera. To know that what I said meets you with obvious inclination.

Though I'm not entirely surprised. The early stages of sentience, be it the phases of a child or the early phases of a combined multitude of lifetimes from having just begun another new cycle of sentience that shall stretch out across eons and eternities of reincarnations… usually maintain this understanding of the natural seeking of the self above all else.

It is usually after such youth and during the later stages of a developing sentience, that this blurs away from common place as the sticky toil begins."

"So I just need to stay strong when that time comes?" asked Vera.

Cornelius shook his head, "No. You just need to remember that the only thing you ever needed to know and ever needed to understand, is yourself. There is no power outside of that. There is no power over you when you have that. There is no other truth.

And with that, never forget that no one and no thing ever *needs* to understand you, except you.

To not fall into the trap of being understood fully by other beings. As if them understanding you to the same whole degree is the same as or even proof of you fully being at one with yourself.

For that path of striving for their perception or their awareness of you… will only lead you into unknowingly falling into a mold during that pursuit of cementing an external view, perception, validation, or agreement with who you are.

Be boundless, Vera. Do not be limited or held down by any mold given to you by anything, even if it is handed to you by the universe itself.

Allow me, Vera, a monster for being boundless, to deliver to you a boundless truth.

For you will be told by many people and many beings— by both those who love you and those who believe in you— that you can be *anything* you want to be.

However, they will only be delivering half of the truth with those words. They will be nearly correct and almost complete by such inspiring, motivational, and supporting words… but such a phrase is so limiting and they can only deliver it as such for they themselves are also limited.

The truth is, with no limits, coming from a boundless being and something which I wish for you to carry for the rest of your life, lives, and sentient phases, is **not** that you can be *anything* you want— it is that you can be **everything** you want.

Be the most delicate of blues if you want: soft in kindness, generous with advice, abundant with love, and tempered with endless patience.

Be the most robust of reds if you desire: fierce in boundaries, deadly in wrath, and heavy handed in judgement.

Be the most royal of purples: sophisticated in character, elegant in poise, and one of a kind in essence.

Be the most common of grays: relatable to all, equal to everything, and indifferent to everyone.

Be the most glorious of gold: radiant in self worth, glowing with self love, and shining with incomparable value.

Whatever it may be, whatever it is you wish to become, *be it all*— not just one.

Be everything you want, not just anything."

Vera nodded, "I understand."

"I am pleased. Now…" began Cornelius, leaning back into his chair while falling into a more relaxed aura, "I said my part and answered your question… in rather long detail, if I might add.

Your answer needn't be as long, but I do expect it to be as thorough in full closure.

So, Vera, who are you? And how did you end up in this realm to cross my path?"

Vera straightened her posture in her seat to respond, as if her answer had been rehearsed and ingrained into her, "My name is Vera Ashen " she began, "Daughter to Priscilla Ashen, High Priestess of the Phoenix Standing, the witching order of the purging flame. Daughter to Fredrix Godless, Patron of the Infraction Tribe, those who give faith to the gods but belong to no order of fixed worship."

"Phoenix Standing?" noted Cornelius with intrigue, "Ah! I see now.

It seems you and I hail from the same realm, Vera Ashen. And not just the same realm, but the same world within it. We just come from different time points along it.

To simplify my expression since time is a complex matter that is nearly impossible to explain to someone who doesn't yet have the capacity to understand such workings: You are from the past, and I, the future."

"You are from a time beyond my current happenings?" asked Vera.

"Indeed I am. Extremely far beyond your time, in fact. You wouldn't even recognize the world anymore should you see it from my original birth point."

"Do you know who wins the War of Standings, then?" asked Vera, her eyes opening wide in anticipation.

Cornelius shook his head, "No.

I did not stay long enough to witness every moment pass nor watch every event occur.

Truly, it's difficult to explain, but think of it as a bird flying over the land. The bird can see it all in the exact order below it— clear enough to map it out, even. But to know the exact details of the happenings in those sections of geography, then the bird must land on the ground like any creature to see it from that perspective.

I have made myself well versed enough with our world's history and the true history of mankind, that I am aware of the time and happenings when I hear something like the 'Phoenix Standing', or 'The War of Standings'... however, when presented with names such as Priscilla Ashen or Fredrix Godless, or asked about the outcome of a specific event— I do not know.

There are many names, faces, and souls of just the humans alone that have spanned the timeline of our single world in our single realm. And trust me when I say that there were just as many wars and still are ones going on even in my own time."

Vera fell silent after hearing this.

"I understand now" said Cornelius, re-sparking the conversation, "But I need you to say it yourself.

Please, continue Vera.

How did you get here?

How did we cross paths?"

"The War of Standings has been going on for a very long time" continued Vera, "Since before my mother's mother.

Every witch fights in a piece of it. And as of right now, there is no foreseeable future to its end.

I actually didn't think it would ever end at all until I met you and you told me what you said just now.

It's a relief to know that it does... but scary to not know which Standing wins.

More men of tribes have been pulled into the war and brought into the efforts of different Standings.

My mother… my father… they seek an end to the war. Most tired minds do, although some live for this war.

My parents see me as the thing that can end it… but I don't know why, and I especially don't know how.

It was by the knowledge of my father, Patron of the Infraction Tribe, that this realm was my destination— as he was told by one of the many gods he speaks to that this place would soon be visited by a being unlike any other.

And it was by the powerful magick of my mother, High Priestess of the Phoenix Standing, that I was sent here before that being's arrival— as only she has the capabilities to touch into other dimensions.

… Is it still considered a rare crossing… if the encounter was planned all along?" she asked, donning a face of innocent guilt.

"I'd say so" answered Cornelius with a warm smile, one that erased Vera's shame that follows any child who anticipates getting in trouble, "In fact, I'd say it's more rare, now.

It is rare for beings to cross my path, but it is even more rare for them to intentionally plan it."

"I'm sorry for deceiving you earlier…" said Vera, "… When I pretended to be lost and meek.

It is true that I don't know my way around this realm, it is foreign to me. But it is by no accident that I am here."

Cornelius laughed, "I know, Vera.

I suspected there was more to you than meets the eye the moment I noticed your presence.

Of all things that lie and deceive— the soul is not one of them.

It was obvious that you were a human child, just as much as it was obvious you were no ordinary one.

Had you been a simple lost mortal, then I probably wouldn't have even come across your bones, as those monsters that once paraded in the fog before I arrived would have undoubtedly feasted upon your flesh.

But they did not, for they could sense the same power and danger you present like I do now. A power and danger of your powerful and dangerous soul, the same soul that made your parents believe you to be the one to end The War of Standings— even if that required the extra edge of encountering a being that could give you some extra knowledge or guidance in doing so.

However... I am not that being, or at least not in the way you think.

Take my words from our conversation and use them how you wish, but know they have everything to do with you— not with The War of Standings."

"Were my parents wrong, then?" asked Vera, "About The War of Standings? About what I would find here? About me?"

Cornelius shrugged, "It depends on what you want, Vera. Your power should be found because it is *your* power and belongs to no one else. It is something to be actualized at one point in your life or cycle of sentience, eventually. Therefore, the drive should not come from a desire to stop The

War of Standings, as that will only make you fall into the cycle of the game.
It must be for nothing else and for no one else other than yourself.

So many beings push it off, get lost in the game, become overwhelmed
and crowded with other things or dogma that they never accomplish it...
despite having all of eternity.

But if you ask me, then I'd say a time of war, a time of strife, a time of
hardship, evil, sadness, or struggle is just as good a time as any— if not the
most vital time —to work towards achieving your own true unity... for then
those evil things that touch your life no longer can.

And if you choose to put an end to The War of Standings after you come
into the fullness of yourself, then so be it. You can completely do so and will
be able to.

You see, the fear other beings have towards monsters is not because of
the ripples we cause, but because of our power to make a ripple disappear.

Absolute oblivion. True elimination of essence and an absence to what
once existed. It can never be found or recycled again, for we do not obey
divine laws. At our will, once something is gone, it's completely disinte-
grated from reality."

Vera gave a weak smile in return to Cornelius' words. She wasn't disap-
pointed in them or their lack of a solution to the immediate problem she was
seeking to solve by encountering him, but she was disheartened to know that
the answer he gave her had no direct connection to it.

And despite his words possibly being true on how to solve it by acquir-
ing her own power, and the fact that reaching such a state would mean The
War of Standings would not even be a priority of concern for her... it still
meant that it was purely on her to reach it. Something only she could do with

no outside aid to speed up the process, lighten the work, or make easier the struggle.

"Before we part ways and you return back to the early days of our realm, Vera, as I'm sure you've always had a way out of here, I want you to take these words with you" said Cornelius, "As a witch, and as the daughter to the High Priestess of the Phoenix Standing: *Make your own fire.*

It will be the first fire to exist.

For although there is already fire and many different kinds of it, there is only *one* of *you*.

Therefore, any fire you create will be *your* fire. The only kind like it— the first fire ever."

Astro Manic: A Mr. Downer Rediscovered

There was a time when humans once told stories about the end of the universe.

They used grandiose examples because, of course, none of them could fathom such a bleak possibility.

They couldn't even comprehend the universe itself, so you can imagine their difficulty in taking it a step further by attempting to depict its end— like the blind leading the blind.

You would hear countless ways in which they tried to take on this colossus challenge, using the most common existential scares to make you feel small, or alone, or meaningless, or perhaps all of the above.

"One day, billions of years from now, the sun of this solar system— our sun —will die. And with it, so will Earth."

"When the last star in this galaxy and the next finally goes out... and the universe goes completely dark. Zero light across the infinite expanse... for all of eternity, until everything grows too cold and dies."

"A sad, empty, and pathetic bubble of black— no longer teeming with life, but merely the scraps of it. And those tenacious beings who, by either biology or spirit, still reside and cling onto the ability to continue their existence, will only be able to do so for a very limited duration. And during that duration, they will wobble around lost, scared, and confused— bumping their heads into each other, waiting to be saved as such a rescue cannot be done by themselves or by their equally discombobulated neighbor."

But the truth is… it **never** required *that* much to feel small, alone, meaningless, lost, scared, or confused.

And in actuality, what the future held for humanity was the complete opposite of those grim yet silly examples, and it remained so for a very long time.

It was inevitable that humans would eventually colonize the entire universe— even with its constant growth and expansion —making this larger than life concept now something which they could easily understand.

It was inevitable that by both integration with machine and a further development of spirituality, that the intricate structures of so many qualities and mechanics which create the foundation of life, the universe, and keeps its gears turning perpetually, or allows us to experience it ourselves, would eventually became understandable and within our capacity for contemplation— making it that much smaller of a truth and something no longer outside of ourselves, but rather, in the very palm of our hands.

And by our new equal standing with that which was once beyond our scope, that which once marked the pinnacle of absolution should we ever evolve by natural or artificial means to conquer it, that which marked the last standing for mankind to dominate and achieve our full potential as sentient beings in this abstract construction of reality, space, and time… now meant that the ideas and concepts which were once used to allude to the emotions and sensations of feeling small, alone, meaningless, lost, scared, and confused… were that which made us feel such a way in the most simple and common of circumstances.

Such as a place once populated now vacant.

A setting once crowded now empty.

A space once noisy now silent.

A community once large now gone.

And an area once bustling now still.

These simple features and these singular differences are all it takes for the autonomy of being purely yourself… all by yourself… to seep into the crevices of one's soul.

A true mastery of the self will incorporate the discipline of being immune to the sensation of feeling abandoned when one is utterly alone and isolated. For it is extremely natural for a person to conceive the notion, or rather, attach to it, that their solitude is related to some deeper alienation.

And this special story in particular bears all of these topics which I have just mentioned as part of its glorious introduction: The end of the universe; man and the colonization of the stars; man and machine; man and spirit; isolation; and a man who mastered himself, and therefore, was immune to the poisons of solitude.

Here at the end— during the end of the end —lies before us, planet Mox.

A radiant planet in terms of social life, culture, organic flow, and mutual living.

However, mutual living does not mean that all were equal on this planet... but it does mean that all types of classes, people, and workers were all shoulder to shoulder for the most part.

For you see, in mankind's expanse into the stars— when every planet, galaxy, and solar system is at their choice of mercy —it is only natural and logical for a whole planet to serve a singular purpose.

Whole planets used and designed for vacations.

Whole planets used and designated for the mining of resources or perhaps a singular resource.

Whole planets that are only occupied with workers who construct and push out the most valuable or widely consumed products by gargantuan mass and in ceaseless flow.

Whole planets for farming, be it a single crop or a multitude of them.

Whole planets for training and creating soldiers adept for any scenario or environment.

It was extremely common for whole planets to serve a singular purpose which in turn served the entire expanse of civilization, just as much as it was for whole planets to serve and maintain the living population only on the planet itself with no service to any other outside it.

There were countless pros and countless cons to each of those variations of planets that existed.

But a planet like Mox... now that felt like something more akin to the old world— like straight from a time before the Astro Manic Era.

So many different things of different value— or even senseless in value —were crowded on its surface and buried beneath its upper crust.

There were large unpopulated areas for farming, and large hyper-populated areas for living and economic circulation. And even within those areas that were condensed with life, there were multiple subdivisions of localized efficiencies or sections for haphazardry.

A true cumulation of life and all of its unique strands, so close to each other despite their vastness in differences and despite all of their obvious inequalities in circumstances— which paradoxically made them all equal in a sense. A rare beauty which can only be observed in the blossom of such positive chaos... something which was easily forgotten in this Astro Manic Era.

And touching down on this planet now was a man— a pure human, one without a single drop of nanos in his blood, no artificial abruption to his DNA, and no augmentation or modifications done to his body.

Few knew who he was. Even fewer knew his story. And yet... everyone had heard a tale of his existence, though it passed around more as a fable similar to folklore of the old world.

But he was very much real and without any injustice to the mystery that surrounded him.

This man was very familiar with the planet Mox. He was actually quite fond of it and every other planet like it during this age, because it reminded him of the old world, a time which the history books, religious texts, and philosophical dogmas of this era could never fully capture despite their references to it and logs of the past.

You see, this man had been alive for a very, very… very long time. He was *naturally* immortal— the first and only human to be born that way. So, unlike everyone else, it was mere memory that connected him to an age now passed. And because he held all the time in the world, he had managed to touch base with almost every planet that existed in the universe— even the barren ones, even the ones he wasn't welcomed on, even the ones which would've resulted in his death should his presence had been discovered, even the ones that he shouldn't have survived walking on as their terrain and electrical grid was built purely for nonorganic intelligences to traverse.

But with all that being said, this was the first time Planet Mox had ever stood so quiet, so still, and so empty for him.

Climbing out of his rig, the man hopped down onto the rooftop which it hovered over, landing with heavy feet and proceeding to walk to its edge where he observed the vacant city that sat before him.

"These neon lights will never die" said the man to himself, his voice distorted from the helmet he wore, *"Truer words have never been spoken."*

Speaking to himself was a common occurrence for the man. In fact, over his eons of existence, he had probably spoken more to himself in casual manner than he had to anyone else in every conversation he's ever had combined.

"But all great cities shall turn to dust" he said while lifting a single hand into the air above his head, brushing it against the gusting wind with a curling of his fingers, "This one's still filled with the particles of life which so recently kept it running."

Sparks and electrical currents flashed at the tips of his fingers during the final motion of his curling fingers from an energetic discharge.

"Hmph" he pulled back his hand and investigated the tips of his fingers, where soot now remained from the burning of old hair and dead skin that still flowed through the air in microscopic particles— now scorched into ash from the brief interaction of an electrical current.

"You must feel the loneliest of all, planet Mox. An entire planet terraformed for both organic and nonorganic life to live upon it.

Having donned the flesh of an electrical current on your surface to breathe life into the technology used by the occupants, as well as to be a stable and consistent fuel source for the nonorganic life itself with that same electricity.

And those organic and nonorganic beings breathed life back into you by tempering that abundance of energy— dampening its surge from their constant consumption of those invisible electric waves.

You kept them up, for they would drown without you.

And they kept you down, for you would over-flood without them.

A true symbiotic relationship. One which most never even realized.

All to be abandoned so suddenly… so *fiercely*. With no clue or reasoning that could ever sedate this flow of energy at your surface.

But perhaps… I can help you with that loneliness you feel, planet Mox.

For I, of all beings, understand."

After surveying the dead city one last time from the vantage point he landed on, the man then began to make his descent down into the lower levels of the building— all while continuing his conversation with the planet Mox as though it could hear him.

"It's a strange thing, loneliness, as I'm sure you've already come to understand, planet Mox.

At its best, it is liberating— sometimes even a sought out thing.

A domain for peace and rapture.

Funny thing about "rapture" is that it has two primary meanings: a noun defining an elated state of bliss and of overwhelming emotion; and in the old world once filled with the old gods and their theology, it was the mythical event involving those who were good people to be taken off the planet and into heaven, while those who weren't good people had to stay on earth and suffer the armageddon.

And that is why rapture is the best way to describe it. For when you are surrounded with bad people— bad meaning simply not good for you in whatever form that may take shape —then separating yourself from them becomes a form of peace.

Isolation becomes the grounds on which a purging and purification can take place on; where a reclaiming of one's energy and identity can be captured; and where the initiation of rebirth can begin its process."

Slowly but surely, the man delved deeper into the lower quarters of the city, and the electrical current which he once felt pulsing throughout his body now began to only quiver within it.

"At its worst, however, loneliness can be crippling— the killer of all hope" he continued, "Like this city and the very building I am traversing, it can go very deep and has many layers, becoming far, **far** worse the deeper you go.

Not all answers work. Not all answers can apply. But there is a commonality— stages, so to say —that are likely to be experienced, but the hole only grows deeper when they do not work.

The first answer is obvious: refill that which you lost.

Be it friends, family, a lover— whether it is a specific person or multiple people, or simply the idea of having such, that is the first solution to be attempted.

Regaining the relationship once lost, or reacquiring a company for a space now vacant.

But if that doesn't work out for any number of valid reasons, then the next stage usually happens, which bears a new answer: setting all intention and energy onto a goal that is disconnected from the isolation… though it can be seen as producing a fruit in the future that happens to solve the problem of isolation organically.

Work, art, education, a project, a hobby, a lost dream, a new passion— it can be any number of things, but it's usually tied to something that requires a level of dedication, commitment, and time, all of which you have in the misty air of unsolved loneliness."

As if the world he was on, planet Mox, was daydreaming to the man's words, the air outside the building began to grow thicker, turning into a fog of the lower levels which he was now entering.

"Sometimes it works. Sometimes it doesn't. Sometimes it never needed to work, as it held off the awareness of you circumstance just long enough for the first solution to make its way over to you and answer the problem unintentionally— commonly known as 'finding that which you desire when you aren't looking for it'.

But if that doesn't work, well then, it's on to the next stage with the new answer: self love.

The mystics of the old world— before the gods were replaced with the new ones who now reign over our universe with an unquestionable presence —would call this phase *'the dark night of the soul'*.

It consists of more than just warm fuzzy feelings, self love.

It forces you to reevaluate *everything*.

How you once felt, how you once perceived, how you once thought, how you once desired— the whole shebang. Everything that makes you… you.

And you *will* come to those deeper understandings of yourself. You *will* realize the things about yourself that you wouldn't trade for the world or even to escape that loneliness, for you value and are proud of the being that you are.

Self love and an internal alignment is achieved at this stage, and so it would seem that a re-emergence into the world to cure that loneliness can finally happen, because you're different, and therefore it will be different this time. Your approach, your search, your idea of what you want and how you will find it— everything.

But sometimes… not even that answers for the solution to the loneliness."

The fog outside began to grow extremely dense from how low to the surface the man now was, blocking out all light from those neon signs cascaded along the neighboring buildings, and casting a pitch black cloak akin to night on the glass windows that looked out.

"Now this, Mox... this is where it gets extremely dangerous.

Here, in these stages, it is nothing but pain, and hurt, and sorrow, and emptiness, and despair.

A dirty cocktail of longing and waiting.

I hope you never reach this stage, planet Mox, for it is a treacherous place that should not exist...and yet, it very well can and it very well does.

A place where when you've done all the healing, all the growth, all the internal changes, and understand yourself in the deepest of ways possible... and yet nothing seems to change.

There's no more work for you to do on yourself. You may still grow, of course, and in fact you'll always continue to grow— but you're now growing from a place of absolute unity within yourself and your being. Just building atop the foundation that has been put in place.

Therefore, there is nothing more you can do, nor are there any realizations left for you to experience that will then result in your situation changing.

For at this level, you are still alone not for any of those reasons, but because it is the other people who haven't changed.

In one way or many, they still exhibit the same things or behaviors which caused you to isolate yourself intentionally or unintentionally in the first place.

There is nothing left for you to do on your end of things in regard to that, for it is out of your control… and yet, you suffer the most because of it.

There's no energy left in you to work on those things outside of the isolation problem anymore, and there is no more motivation to continue working on such things that had once been seen with a great passion by you.

Slowly, they all lose purpose— perhaps they already did a while ago.

The meaning and the fruit of their labor no longer hold the same value, and such things have become so pointless in the whole of it all.

And worst of all… hope has become an enemy— a cruel and bitter thing that seems to only further your torment, when for so long, all you've needed and deserved was a kindness and an act of mercy.

Hope is no longer that light at the end of the tunnel, but a twisted grin of foul tease that will do anything but actually answer your ancient longing for something so simple, so innocent, and so humble… which is just *company*.

Company which you can enjoy with a heart at ease. Company which does right by you. Company which fulfills you. Company which understands you, makes an effort for you, cares for you, considers you, and acknowledges when you do the same for them.

You realize how simple such a desire really is at the core of it all, and that it's not some outrageous or greedy request.

You know, better than all, how this is what makes life worth living, life exciting, life have purpose and meaning.

And yet… it is the thing you lack the most."

The man stopped his descending of floors despite there being many more levels he could go, for it seemed this was the level where he had desired to reach, and the entire reason for his visit to planet Mox.

Lifting his left arm to his face, he began to fiddle with the screen on the black band he wore, causing the dark room to light up in response after a couple of seconds passed.

"The worst part about this stage" continued the man as he walked with a purpose towards a specific location on this floor, "Is that it feels like the solution to your loneliness is completely out of your control... which it is for the reasons already stated.

It's unfair. It doesn't make sense. It's doesn't seem very loving, kind, or logical of the universe to allow for such a thing like this to exist.

And all you're left with is a feeling of abandonment by the universe itself at that point. And why wouldn't you? If everything or anything was just a little bit better, if everyone or anyone was just a bit more decent of a being, a bit more kind... then everything would be different.

And you've paid your dues and done your work and have completed your end of everything that you can on the matter, so now you're just waiting on anyone or someone else to.

It's completely out of your control, which makes it a miracle. And it is the universe who hands out those things.

Mox... I am so utterly sorry to say that when it comes to being trapped in this stage, I have no answer for its solution. I have no lesson or teaching or words that will make it all wash away or make sense. I have no piece for what feels like a hidden puzzle in this stage that can finally grant true change and an escape from it, or a clarity to the bigger picture."

The man entered a random room within the building and approached the wall facing opposite its entry.

Once more he began to fiddle with the screen attached to his left arm, causing a discrete panel of walls to begin to shift in complex orientations— revealing a secret safe behind the wall.

For how intricate the rigged panels were which both hid and protected this secret safe, it was unimpressively small of a box, denoting that whatever it held within it was even smaller.

"However" said the man as he now began his process of cracking open the safe, using both his arm band as well as manual efforts, "What I can offer you is advice— from one being who has been there to another.

I know, I know. Advice is not what you seek, an answer is.

Aiding words is not what you desire, a genuine change is.

But in that dark pit, this advice *will* help you until your miracle comes along.

My first piece of advice: be acutely aware of the fangs that are anger and envy.

Whether you are reflecting on the past, looking at the current, or pondering upon the future, notice when the fangs of anger and envy attempt to release their cloud of poison into those thoughts and observations.

You're already aware of the foul that has touched your trials and tribulations of existence, you have been for a long time. There's no more gold to be transmuted from this lead. It once served you to sit with it and accept the negative facets that surrounded a truth, but no longer does it do the same.

The anger and envy now only serve as a specter of the foul which sur-rounded a truth, like the anchor of a ghost ship, serving no other purpose than to continue pulling you down or keeping you in place, as opposed to fading away like all ghosts should.

You know the things that hurt you and can hurt you in the present, you know them very well and can expound upon them indefinitely from new angles and circumstances. So don't do that. Allow it no longer.

And take confidence in this truth hidden in plain sight— which is because of that very awareness... it is and already has been applied to the future. Rest assured, you will not enter such spaces where that hurt exists, and you will not remain in them should such hurt ever enter it."

Of the four lights that sat above the safe, one chimed in a successful resonance and turned green.

"My second piece of advice: when you do have energy, act on it.

It is important not to push yourself in such a desolate time. Forcing yourself to act on a passion that no longer holds any meaning, or on an idea that you have no motivation for, or towards an outcome that barely retains any of the same value it once did, will do nothing but further exhaust you.

So take rest, be on your own side of understanding, be the gentle embrace of a warm and nurturing figure for yourself which you have wished for so long to fall into. Be the essence you are for others— for yourself. Focus on feeling instead of thinking, and allow yourself to fall into your own energy to alleviate the pressure and wash away all the hurt.

And then, on the rare occasions when you do feel energy, when you do feel motivated, when things be it general or specific have regained a value, purpose, or meaning to you— **act on it**.

Act on it immediately. Whether the energy lasts for a mere moment, a few hours, a whole day, or even a handful of weeks— act on it to the fullest until it subsides."

Another chime rendered its harmonic sound, igniting a second red light to turn green.

"My third piece of advice: remember the sweet nectar of the original fruit.

Before all the pain, before all the hurt, before all the realizations of the corruption that exists or the interferences that can take place or have taken place— before all those things which stale, take away from, lead astray, or stomp out the beauty of a pure and precious thing you once felt and wanted— you were excited at the prospects of those things you once desired.

Remember that time. Remember that awe, and that eagerness, and that excitement, and all those feelings you once felt from the idea of that desire, and the sight of its boundless opportunity and its capacity for that beauty to take on its form in an abundance of numerous ways.

Yes, you have realized, learned, experienced, and saw how such things can be spoiled, and corrupted, and ruined, and how all those things can happen at the hands of others and not even yourself— how they can still be ruined no matter how much you do right by it or present good and true for it.

But do not reflect on yourself as a fool for having once seen it in such a beautiful way and in a pure manner.

You were not naive for seeing the sweet nectar of those fruits long ago— you were powerful and true for seeing them in their purest state.

And wouldn't you say that that specific state of it which excites you the most, which comes with the most ease of heart, which bears the most joyful of sensations, which creates the most happy of an experience and existence, is the truest version to have sought after and still seek now?

What other manner of it would you want?

The real question is, why is any such manner of it that is not that... able to exist? Because it shouldn't.

But sadly, as you've learned, those other versions do exist.

And a common occurrence during that learning process is to then believe that just because these other versions exist, just because something so good and simple and pure can be and is frequently corrupted, that it must mean that the most sacred and pure version of it that you once held real is not real.

That the original way you saw it was a fantasy.

However, that is not true. It is no fantasy.

Just as you were powerful enough to see it in its greatest, truest, and natural form, so too were you powerful enough to witness and identify all the ways in which something so great and pure is corrupted and the ways in which that corruption can occur. But do not let it wash away your original excitement and outlook.

One did not replace the other. They both always existed. At one time, all you saw was the true and pure form of it that excited you. And now, after having experienced the opposite of that and seen all the ways that go against it, you only see the corrupted version.

So remember the sweet nectar of the original fruit. Strive for that *feeling* you once had towards it, as opposed to only keeping sights on achieving an outcome from it."

A third chime dinged and another red light turned green, leaving one last lock to solve.

"And my last piece of advice I have to give: now is the time of knowing, you have far transcended the time of believing.

In all this time, you have grown as a being.

You have become more aware of the type of being you want to be, and strived to become that being in ways both consciously and subconsciously.

And you've seen and noticed these changes, you've realized them and how far you actually are despite how you may look or feel. You know better than to compare that achievement to an outcome you once imagined of how things would look when you achieved them, because you've already learned now not to attach them to the outcome of external factors.

And yet, despite how far you've come… you still feel so far away, because the things you feel don't match up with how you expected, think, or imagined them to feel like once you were fully there and achieved it in its absoluteness.

And that exact fullness of sensations which you have still not yielded to yourself yet is being restrained by still focusing on the aspect of believing.

But you don't need to believe anymore.

Now you need to know it.

Hold the power of knowing that you are, instead of the strength of believing that you are.

They are two separate mountains, knowing and believing.

One is harder to climb— that being the believing. And once you have reached the top of it, it's time for the next one.

The other mountain is harder to see— that being the knowing. But once you realize this, it is an immediate jump to its top— it does not require the same strain and suffering that the mountain of believing required, for the work that it took to reach the top of that mountain is immediately transferred over, for the mountain is the one to change in this situation and it changes beneath your feet.

No longer do you need to believe, for now you get to stand on the knowing."

As the last chime sounded and the final red light turned green, the tiny door of the tiny safe loosely swung open from the lock releasing its solid grip of closure.

In front of the man, lying quietly inside the bed of the safe was a unique necklace.

It was made of a blue crystal of some sort which displayed the perfect shape of a curved tear drop, and bore a long piece of leather string which wrapped and knotted around its tip to hang from one's neck.

"You know something, Mox… monsters existed in the old world just as much as they do now in the Astro Manic Era.

When we think about the nature of monsters, one of the key themes is that they consume us. Despite it not being limited to this, a devouring of sort *is* usually involved in the fable regarding the monster.

That is how most of them are identified as— they seek to eat us.

So it's surprising to see how often those same monsters *within* us are overlooked.

I'm not talking about an evil within us, or our darkest demons coming to the surface. No, nothing like that at all.

I'm referring to everything I just spoke on.

How our emotions can eat us up. How different states of being such as loneliness can swallow us whole. How our hopes and dreams and previous outlooks on things can be devoured by the corruption we bear witness to it, stealing away our excitement and joy that we once felt to the truth and purity of such things.

These monsters are dangerous for they are *invisible*.

They look just like life itself, however, they do not belong... no matter what anyone might say.

We have legends and stories of heroes who slay monsters. However, when it comes to this particular breed of monster, we must strive to be the heroes in our own stories and slay them ourselves... lest we never find the things we desire most or return to the outlook that once made life worth it all and pleasureful."

The man reached into the safe and took out the necklace, unfolding its length and putting it on over his helmet.

"I am happy to say though that I can be a miracle to someone else this time.

It is gratifying to wield such a power, and certainly is easier than the internal strife of having to find it within yourself or wait on someone else. It's a nice break to be someone else's hero.

This necklace is what shall save them. A new world lies entirely on the other side of what's to come, and with this necklace, they shall be able to see it too. We shall see it *together*.

A world and a universe that is finally beyond those trials and tribulations of corruption and monsters. One that has achieved the purity and excitement which we held onto strong within our hearts all this time and pushed to the surface to see the light again despite being in a dark world" the man let out a heavy sigh of relief, "It took so, so, *so* long. Countless years, countless lifetimes, countless eras... and I doubted infinitely whether I'd ever see this day or if it was to actually come at all.

I am so happy and relieved that it's finally here, and the only reason that I was able to last this long, planet Mox, is because of the advice I gave to you.

After an endless loop of eons, my miracle's finally here."

May The Night Take Me Before He

I don't know when this castle was built, but without a doubt, it was meant for many people.

I don't know if it was once filled with life, vigor, and a bustle from many occupants... but now, without a doubt, it should remain empty and still... say for that single soul who roams its many floors.

I have no idea what sort of eyes once looked upon this location when the ground was bear and the cliff stood naked— pristine and untouched as the sun rose above the sea each morning. Surely it seemed like a magical spot, blessed with the salt of the ocean and the golden rays of the sun... but now, it stands here like a dead tree whose roots have petrified itself into place. Dead land from dead soil, it's like the beam of a lighthouse that hauntingly emerges from the fogbank, trapped to this single spot on earth due to an unfinished life of unfulfilled dreams.

I do not know if the creature in this castle with me was once human. If he was a normal man with a normal appearance, perhaps even a sense of charm... but without a doubt, he is now a monster. A monster who wants my blood... and hopefully nothing more.

My name is Alexandra, and I find myself in the castle's attic— a place that usually holds the most gloom of any living space... but here, it acts as the single place of sanctuary to find safety.

It's a miracle I managed to make my way up here in the first place, for as I stated earlier, this castle has many levels. And although I am safe in this single room that makes up the entirety of this upper quarter... I am also trapped— a prisoner to the safety that keeps me alive, for I haven't been able to leave.

The creature that occupies this tomb of a castle with me is a monster... or to be more specific, he is a vampire.

I had heard the tales of such blood thirsty beasts when I was a little girl. I heard all the stories about them like any child is told, and even more grim ones when I became older from the odd souls who dabbled in the darker aspects of the world.

However, none of their descriptions match up with this vampire. And even if they had, none of their warnings of its behavior could've prepared me for the strong grasp of desperation that takes hold after such an encounter.

Shock has long since left my body, and even the dramatics of fear which consumes one's heart has eased away to a degree.

Now, all I am left with is an exhausted instinct to survive, one based more in common self-preservation than fear.

I no longer fear dying— I fear not making it out of this place.

I no longer fear the vampire in the hallways— I fear specifically losing my life *to* it.

It may be a gruesome or even perverted death at his hands, so I fear the pain that would ensue should he be the one to kill me before starvation does.

And so I pray every night... that the night may take me before he.

But prayers require a voice, and even the tiniest motion of the lips allow air into my mouth. So after many days of this, my throat has become too dry to continue with these prayers or to rely on the mercy of an unseen savior.

Which is why I plan to make my escape today.

It'll have to be successful. It *must* be successful.

For anything short of it... would mean he has caught me.

If you're curious on what this vampire looks like, I will tell you.

The most noticeable thing upon first sight of it, is that the creature is blue. A deep but gentle blue, like that of a blue morpho butterfly.

Its skin is glossy and ever smooth like a slug, reflecting light off its body to reveal every curve, bump, and dip in its flesh from the bones and muscles beneath it.

Its forearms are ungodly long, and at the end of them lie abnormally large hands with thick curved nails— pure black.

Its body— both torso and legs —are also elongated, making the creature tall and elegant like a ballet dancer. It's quite disturbing to watch something so evil move with such a surplus of grace.

Its face holds much resemblance to that of a man, but the features are too emphasized and dramatic in certain areas to make it anything but human. Even the ugliest man could not produce the disgruntling effect that this vampire's visage enforces upon its looker.

And its teeth are no different to its nails— abnormally large, pointed sharp, and pure black. In fact, it is from how large its teeth are that fill up its mouth which causes the uncanny impression upon its face. The way the skin is stretched over the extended maxilla to keep the lips touching and mouth closed... it is not a natural look by any being I have happened upon.

I think the creature speaks, but I cannot be certain.

Sometimes I hear it make noises, like mumbles or groans, but they are clustered together so I question whether the creature is stitching together words from a language that I maybe do not know.

Undoubtedly there is an intelligence within the creature's mind, but its sinister soul creates a valley between us in understanding— therefore, I can only perceive the vampire as a mindless beast who wishes me harm.

If I was a witch who was more familiar with the darker arts, or maybe even a bad person who knew of evil thoughts, then maybe there would be a space between me and this creature for at least a strained level of communication.

I know what you're thinking... *"I've never heard of a vampire like that".*

And to that I'd say— of course you haven't.

There's a reason you, and I, and all the others who told us the stories of vampires have never encountered one like this before... and that is because none would have lived to tell of it.

I bet there are actually many who have encountered this breed of evil before... they just never had a chance to survive and warn of it.

But I am confident that I can be the first.

Having been in this attic with nothing but my own thoughts have allowed my nerves to return to me, something I don't believe the 'possible others' may have had the luxury of.

And with that return of my nerve, so too has a strength entered my body which I never knew existed.

There are multiple windows and stained glass decorating these slanted walls and ceiling of this attic. It is the sole reason for my safety.

During the day, light shines brightest in this room. And during the night, it is no different, for the moon reflects with a strong silver glare in here from that distant sun shining on the opposite side of the world.

This room must've burnt the beast multiple times during both the day-time and the night, hence it never dares to enter.

Since I cannot be assured that the levels and rooms below this one will have the same effect, I've decided to wait until first sunrise to depart from this attic and make my way down the lower floors.

I have also taken extra measures to conceal my scent.

I believe that the beast can smell me— inferred by the many tales I've been told of vampires and the familiarities I've put together from across all of them. Yes, this vampire is not like the ones I've heard of, but perhaps that doesn't completely exempt it from a share of similarities to its cousins, as it has proved to hold a common theme with them in regards to the sun.

With this in mind, I have swapped out of my dress for one of the older garments I have found stored in this attic. It fits decent enough, but the style is not to my taste.

I'm hoping that the old dry scent from this dress will shroud my own, and that by leaving my old one in here which I have worn for the last several days that I've been trapped, I will succeed in providing the illusion that I am still in the attic as it bears my smell the strongest.

... This vampire is intelligent however, so I only intend to fool the creature briefly. Hopefully with my primary scent still bearing strongest in the attic, it will dissuade the vampire's interest in any faint trace of it that follows me around the castle. At best, the creature might believe that I merely roamed the halls during the day, but then retreated back to the attic before night.

This is all in preparation for the worst event, of course— such as me not succeeding in leaving this place before night falls again.

I hope it does not take me so long, but I will not put my life in meaningless jeopardy should that happen.

I have already removed the old furniture that I stacked over the floor door's entrance as a barricade, and now, with the golden aura of the sun rising above the ocean— flooding my space and sending colors dancing through the stained glass... it is time for me to begin my escape.

Upon opening the floor door that led to the level below me, I was immediately hit with the sour scent of the castle which I had completely forgotten about.

It was pungent and sharp, reminiscent of dried vomit.

This revolting aroma was something I had connected to the creature, as it came off the vampire and always followed it in a slow linger, allowing me to know what rooms it was recently in whenever the beast wasn't present.

This smell let me know that the creature had idly waited outside of the attic during the night, and my decision to leave it and escape during the morning was smart.

I cast down the wooden ladder and climbed downwards, saying goodbye to my haven of protection once and for all.

This level of the castle was quite barren.

I peeked into the numerous rooms while sneaking around towards the staircase, but they were all insignificant— bearing empty rooms except for some carpets, miscellaneous furniture covered in tarps and dust, old art from a forgotten time bearing portraits of lost figures— possibly related to this castle or the land's history —and some random pieces of debris… like broken pieces of the castle that were once damaged and removed but now sat here motionless awaiting restoration.

When I reached the giant staircase, I cautiously made my way down with slow and intentional steps.

The wooden planks were cold, and my heart fluttered every time one of them responded to my weight with a creak or crunch.

It felt more intense coming down those first flight of stairs than it did exiting the attic, but I managed to make it successfully to another level lower once again.

This hall was much different than the previous one, being more reminiscent to a living quarter than an empty one for storage.

The walls were decorated with art; iron-cast candle holders clung bold in measured distance from each other; the windows at the end of the hallways bore elegant drapes above them; and the rooms were filled with beds that varied in their size or quantity.

There was nothing significant to be found in any of them... though that's not to say that I was looking for anything in particular. But I did find myself consumed with an urge to check each one briefly, oddly enough.

I don't know why or what I thought could be discovered by this extra meticulous process... perhaps this sensation was spawned by an unknown instinct in my subconscious— that to sprint all the way down through the halls and stairs was too easy of an escape, too easy of a solution to what seemed impossible for so long, or could've prevented all the hunger, thirst, and strife I endured in that attic.

Maybe deep down I had a fear that upon reaching the main door of the castle to escape, I would be met with locked latch or some sort of blockade to keep me in, similar to how I had the attic door covered to keep the creature out. And upon seeing such a sight, I would have doomed myself to demise since I relied on the main entrance to be my only escape, and had I just checked the rooms on my way down beforehand, then I could've more swiftly conducted an alternative plan from what was once an insignificant discovery now turned miraculous.

But regardless of whether this was a smart precaution or not, this floor did not provide me with any such thing or piece of knowledge that could aid in a compromised future dilemma... so I continued on to the stairs and went down another level lower.

Without a doubt, this section of the castle was obviously used during the time it once hosted life.

The decor was finer, paintings grander, cold melted candles still occupied their iron thrones, tapestry and drapes bore gilded threads, and the rugs had a subtle faintness to them derived from the prolonged traction of people once walking across them frequently.

The rooms on this level were no different than its hall in terms of elegance, as they all contained single master beds upon majestic hand-carved wood frames.

With the contents of these rooms visibly bearing more fruit, or rather, the possibility of something significant being hidden inside them, I decided to fully enter one.

The first thing that stood out to me was how disheveled the space was. It was by no means messy or unkept, but definitely misaligned in a particular way that reflected a past struggle that must have taken place in this room.

For example, the rug that spanned across the floor beneath the bed was lifted, curled, and grooved in random places— like sporadic movement had upset that which should've been a smooth and tidy layout.

The dresser was not aligned straight with the wall, but rather, slightly angled out by a degree… as though someone bumped into the heavy piece of furniture… or perhaps was thrown into it.

The candle holder was on the ground beside the nightstand, and the nightstand itself bore a giant crack running down the middle of it, even through the drawers— like a clean shock of force split the face of the wood from a single impact.

And the drapes of this room laid on the floor, ripped from the rings they were once attached to above the window.

Before I could finish my full survey of the room, I noticed an open door connected to this master bedroom bearing a lavatory.

All thoughts and concerns ceased as I immediately sprinted towards it, placed my head into the ceramic bowl of a sink, and then turned on the faucet.

I didn't even have time to think or rationalize how such a decrepit and rundown castle could still have a running water system, as I was too consumed with the primal urge to drink, and filled with the gratifying sensation of my thirst being quenched.

Slowly, with each gulp, it felt like I was emerging out of a fog that I hadn't realized was screened over my conscious of awareness.

As the thirst died down from my continuous drinking, a new clarity began to blossom.

When I finally desired no more water, I splashed some on my face and took a couple of breaths to reground myself in what felt like a new awakening.

Though I felt better now, I also felt more sick. I think the feeling of illness came from the deeper realization of my situation, which I was now able to better understand with this new sensation of a mental capacity that I had achieved from rehydration.

The knots in my stomach that once kept me sealed in the attic now returned in full strength, but I knew these emotions didn't keep me safe— they kept me trapped.

Turning off the faucet, I stepped out of the lavatory and back into the master bedroom.

I was planning to immediately leave the room and continue my circuits around the castle down to the lower levels... but felt a draw of curiosity towards the bed in this room when I realized that the canopy encircling it was closed shut.

And then I wondered... *"Does the monster sleep in this bed? Behind the shadows of its shut canopy?"*

It wasn't a foolish thought, I promise. But it was bodacious. For three large windows sat on the walls of this room with their drapes on the floor, and sunlight filled its space like a fearless saint who does not bend to evil.

To think that I would no longer be running, but rather, act as the very demise of this creature... well, that swayed my entire spirit into one of confrontation.

Like a beautiful story rooted in cliché, crafted from the universe that tells of a prey turned into the predator.

So cautiously, I crept towards the bed until I stood at arms'-length from it.

I reached out and grabbed a piece of the fabric that draped over its four corners, and without any pause or hesitance, I pulled it open with ferocity!

...

Why my bravery only stood with the idea of the monster being behind the canopy— asleep upon the bed —I have no idea. For that would seem to be the most frightening outcome to any soul in my predicament.

And yet, it was not the monster that lay in the bed behind the curtains... therefore, a fear that accompanies shock and surprise was still able to possess me.

For lying atop the master bed was a skeleton— dried bones frozen in a state of agony despite there being no flesh to show it.

This empty corpse was once a woman. There's no doubt about that. For despite all the organic makeup except her bones having faded away with time... her clothes did not.

And what she wore was a dress very similar to mine— the one which I found in the attic and donned to hide my scent.

Shocked, repulsed, and terrified, I frantically jolted back from the scene in front of me.

However, my bare heel caught on a piece of the lifted carpet beneath my feet, causing my jolt backwards to become a stumble, my stumble to become a fall, and my fa—

⇥⬤ ⬤⇤

I do not understand what this sensation is.

My head hurts. It comes in random pulses and throbs, aching the core of my mind.

Wait... I recognize it now— this is pain.

I was confused moments ago, but now I am not.

I recognize the source for my disorientation— I was unconscious.

I didn't know where I was or what I was doing in those first few moments of waking up, but now I remember— I realize what has happened that has caused my current predicament.

Lifting my face from off the floor, and pushing my chest up off the ground, I observed and acknowledged that I am in one of the master bedrooms of the castle— the room where I drank water from the lavatory and discovered a skeleton in the bed.

I rubbed the back of my head in response to another pulse of sheer pain that throbs my tender skull, and am met with a giant knot on the spot of agony.

Glancing behind my shoulder, I identify the piece of furniture— a giant dresser carved from thick, dense wood —that is responsible for knocking me out when I fell backwards.

Honestly, all I want to do is sleep right now.

I am so tired.

But I can't because of these throbs of pain.

I try closing my eyes and hoping that the aches will cease long enough for me to fall back asleep... but they always return un-rythmically and unsuspectingly— forcing me to wince my eyes and then inconveniently open them to steady my vision on a pattern on the carpet, as the steady concentration helps me drown out the pain.

This cycle continued on and on until I could no longer focus in on a random pattern in the carpet, for the room grew too dark for the imagery to stand out.

... Wait.

... No!

I've forgotten!

I've forgotten too much!

The light!

I need the light!

How could this have slipped my mind!?

How long was I unconscious from hitting my head? How many hours did I waste away asleep? How many precious moments did I throw away trying to tame my headache?

How could I have forgotten the one thing that means my life?

Have I damned myself?

Night is falling and I am nowhere near my escape, let alone the safety of the attic.

Do I have time to run back up into it? Should I just sprint down the stairs towards the entrance? Should I barricade this room closed and hope the creature doesn't draw near?

Which course of action is the best one to ta—

. . .

Oh no.

I hear him.

I smell him.

He is approaching.

His foul scent has crept its way onto this floor. And his strange dialect of murmurs and growls can be heard drawing closer in the hallway— approaching towards this very room.

I was out of time. Out of time for any of those previous options.

There were no thoughts now— just feelings.

And I felt like a tiny bug in a very large and dangerous world.

So, like such, my body took on a mind of its own and crawled without premeditation to a place I could hide.

Under the bed, encased by an even darker shadow than the one that consumed the whole room now that the sun had fully set, I hid.

I dared not to make any sound nor movement as I watched the entrance of the room where the vampire slowly walked in— a plopping sound accompanying his normally quiet feet... as though the elegance he once carried in his gait was now replaced by a boldness not much unlike my own in the fleeing of the attic.

His stench began to flood the room like its own cloud of dread, the pungent odor only intensifying as the vampire made his way towards the bed and stopped at its edge... his legs mere inches from my face.

He continued muttering more of that foreign tongue of odd vowels and drones, indistinguishable from whether he was speaking to himself or perhaps to me if he did know I was here in the room.

Then, I heard the rough sound of cracks and pops, followed by a disgusting noise of the beast slurping and sucking and swallowing.

... He was breaking open the bones of the corpse on the bed and attempting to suck up the dust of any dry marrow within them.

This realization actually brought me some relief, as it told me that the vampire could not clearly distinguish my scent just yet from the successful swapping of dresses in the attic, and his confusion to the faint traces of life he smelt was rationalized as there being some sustenance left that still remained inside the empty skeleton of the one who was decomposed on the bed.

The snaps and slurps continued on for only a few more moments, and then the monster left the way he came.

I listened intensely to the direction which he left in, and felt even more satisfaction in recognizing that he was following the path towards the ascending stairs for the attic— leaving me a clear opening for the stairs heading downwards.

With a balance of caution and haste, I emerged out of my hiding spot from under the bed and snuck into the hallway— heading straight for the descending stairs to the lower levels.

I stayed on the balls of my feet the whole time, my heels never touching the floor for an instant.

I breathed shallowly and controlled, never inhaling too loud or exhaling too abrupt.

My ears felt like a cat's, as though they moved both forward and backward to face any sound that came from any direction.

I was on guard. And I knew the stakes of any failure would be my life.

I did not stick to my original plan of checking every room on the way down, but instead, continued down the stairs zealously— hoping for the front entrance of the castle to provide me my freedom.

I had made it down four more levels with only three more to go to reach the main floor… when I heard the monster speak from the upper levels.

It wasn't a shout or a bellow, but more of an announcement— a loud projection of its voice meant not to scare nor to reflect any rage, but rather, to address me in a manner in which I would hear it.

… *The creature knew I was no longer in the attic.*

It had pieced it together, and in its foreign language, told me so from the upper levels where it had this epiphany.

I do not know exactly what the beast said, just like how it didn't know exactly where in the castle I was. I just knew that its strange words were letting me know that it discovered the truth of my trickery, just as it knew that I was no longer hiding myself in the attic.

Immediately I broke into a sprint down the stairs, abandoning all the previous subtlety and subterfuge I coveted.

Panic surged, horror drew, nausea rippled, and all hope scurried from my body as I bounded down the last levels of the castle.

At times, it felt as though my feet couldn't keep up with the fleeing of my soul, and in turn, I would catch myself skipping stairs by the handful— leaping and nearly tripping down five whole stairs and large gaps at a time.

The adrenaline dulled my ankles from the pain of this, but I knew that they were either badly bruised or fully broken by the time I reached the main floor.

This mattered not, however, as I could still stand on them and move at a normal speed, and I was willing to deal with any damage or suffering that came with their healing as long as it took place in a future where I was out of this castle, and this was all just one ugly nightmare far behind me.

As I sprinted through the large corridors and past all the grand rooms for serving company and entertaining guests, I could see the tall wooden doors of the main entrance ahead of me.

There was nothing propped in front of the doors to prevent me from using them, and despite my frantic charge, all seemed calm and normal at the front entrance.

I slammed into those thick wooden panels to stop my momentum as I was unable to slow myself down, then immediately began pulling on their frames.

… But they didn't budge.

There was zero give of any kind, absolutely no movement or change to their wall-like structure in opening or surrendering any access to the outside world and away from this cursed fort.

An amused laugh sounded from behind me, echoing all the way back from the corridors where the flight of stairs were.

He had already caught up and reached the bottom ground floor.

His speed, despite being fast, was still relaxed in manner as the vampire held no concern regarding my escape.

The front entrance was locked— possibly by a spell of some sort from its deep rooted closure. And if I was to guess, I'd say it was probably closed in such a manner on the first night I spent in the attic.

The beast was never worried about me escaping from the beginning. Not even for an instant.

Because for the immortal creature, it was only a matter of time before I exited the attic to try my luck at departing the castle. And with all the time in the world, waiting for me to do so was never a task or a trial for it.

Patience was never a virtue for this thing— *it was a given.*

I bolted from the locked door and into the adjacent rooms nearby, dashing through them mindlessly with no clear direction other than forward. No real plan other than away.

But I came face to face with my fate when I ended up in the kitchen… a room with no more doors to perpetuate my eternal sprint.

Besides the abundant cookware and cobwebs that littered this room, there was only a chained gate to the basement for wine which was locked… and a large cabinet-sized window which overlooked the ocean as it faced the edge of the cliff that this castle stood on.

The moon was high in the sky and blared down a large silver ray through this glass. This made the room bright like the attic, and I wondered if it held any of the same safety of it as well.

I decided to place myself in the moonlight in hopes that it might, and then braced myself for the vampire to finally catch up to me in his leisurely follow.

It only took seconds to pass before I could smell the creature nearing, accompanied by the sound of his strange murmurs.

In response to the kitchen being more lit by the moonlight let in through the window, the vampire slowly rounded himself around the doorway and into the room like a shy child who was leaving the safety from behind their mother's leg while in front of a stranger.

His fixation on me, however, granted him a boldness and an audacity which he previously lacked to enter the attic since I was now visibly in front of him, and he approached me as close as he could without daring to step into the actual beam of silverlight that showered from behind me.

His eyes menacingly peered into mine while he continued his ramblings of enigmatic language... until they glanced down and noticed the dress I was wearing.

In that moment, I saw a flicker in his eyes as they recognized the piece of apparel, which softened their intensity into something resembling that more of a human than a monster.

And I felt a softening in his spirit, replacing the once predatory aura with one that was considerably more familiar in terms of human emotion— like that of a heart.

Even his energy must have changed, for in that moment I understood what the witches meant when they spoke about the importance of intention, as I was now able to understand the creature as it talked despite its words still being that of a foreign language.

"My love..." said the vampire, *"You've come back!"*

The excitement and heartache could be just as much felt as they were heard— as if the emotions were my own.

"I'm— I'm so sorry.

"I tried. I tried to fix all of it, but I keep falling into the curse of this knowledge.

It was for us, remember?

It was for our sake!

You gave me the courage. Remember when you took me by the hand... then looked into my eyes and sai— "

The vampire looked up from my dress and back into my eyes as if replaying the memory he was enchanted by, and upon doing so... was confronted with mine. My eyes, which did not belong to the woman who he once loved, the woman who once owned this dress. Eyes which threw him back into the reality of this current situation— returning him to his previous state of mind and aura... only this time... with rage.

The creature's energy fluttered back into its nefarious state, writhing with anger and hate now, and following in suite, I could no longer understand or translate his tongue anymore.

But it did not take an intention of energy for me to know that the words which flailed out of his mouth with spit from their ferocity were that of insult and betrayal to my wearing of his former lover's dress, as well as for the vulnerability which he fell into for a brief moment.

Sensing his malice and hostility, a grabbed an iron pan that sat on a counter beside me and held it close like a shield.

However, this made me angry at myself, for it reflected the same choices which had kept me trapped in the attic— a feeble defense out of a belief that I could not fight.

And just like how I refused to stay in the attic, I refused to not fight now, and I refused to let this beast take me.

I thought once more to myself with the utmost resolve, *"May the night take me before he…"* then pivoted on my feet to face the grand window behind me.

I hurled the iron pan through its glass framing, shattering it all into a thousand little pieces.

As a cold air blew in with the strength of the sea's horizon behind it, I embraced that chilly wind and the dark void of the ocean by leaping out of the broken window and flying off the cliff's edge.

It felt like I was falling for minutes, though in reality it had only been seconds.

It was a strange sensation of being suspended in the air. My mind felt like it was free floating while my body catapulted downwards towards the water.

It felt like freedom!

Like this whole time, the condition for my freedom was always going to be such a radical action, and was never as simple as leaving the same way in which I came in.

With a large boom and a hard pound on my feet, followed by an icy piercing upon my skin and a pitch black void of consumption, I submerged into the water from reaching the end of my fall.

I was disoriented in a similar manner from when I had knocked myself unconscious earlier, only this time I never fully blacked out.

And without wasting the awareness I was still able to maintain this time, I frantically swam up to the surface— guided by the large moon's glow on the other side of the water.

My head popped up and I began gasping for air, coughing up the residual water which I had swallowed during the initial chaos.

I observed my surroundings— the moonlight bright enough to make the environment visible despite it being nightfall —and began swimming around the protruding rocks surrounding the cliff which I had just narrowly avoided by chance upon my landing.

I swam more outward into the ocean, hoping that the distance would allow me to see a shore that I could climb up on since most of the area was steep cliff that acted as a wall to contain the ocean.

But for some odd reason... I could still feel the vampire's rage even from outside the castle... even while within these freezing cold waters... even while this far out into the sea.

I looked up to the top of the cliff— to that very edge where the castle stood —and standing at the open mouth of the broken window which I had just jumped out of... now loomed the dark creature as it watched me from afar.

I don't know what I expected, I don't know what I thought... it was all foolish though, for I believed that the beast was bound to the castle.

Oh how terribly wrong I was.

My stomach twisted and all blood sank to my feet when I saw the monster leap down from the window and into the ocean... just as I did.

It bore grace in its dive though, no different than how it bore elegance in its walk.

And all of time stood still after the pound sounded of its body clashing into the water.

I was left only with the unappealing noise from my own heavy breathing as I waited for the creature to pop up... or to pull me under.

Then, breaking all the tension of anticipation, the monster burst from beneath the surface of the water it was once under and began swimming towards me with incredible speed.

It had powerful and athletic butterfly-strokes that propelled it through the water. And in a matter of mere seconds it had already closed half of the distance between us.

I wondered in those few moments that I had left before it was on me, whether a death by the vampire in the sea would be more gruesome or more merciful than a death by it in the castle.

Surely he was limited in the extent to which he could act against me while we both sat in this large body of water... but even if it was only death that should stand as my interaction with him now, would the act of simultaneously drowning make it bear more suffering?

These thoughts mattered not, however, for the truth of how this would all play out was about to be known by pure experience.

I did not want to go into the eternal darkness of death with my last memories being of only darkness as well, so I decided to keep my eyes open courageously throughout my final moments, and watched bravely as the vampire neared.

Woosh!

The sound was oddly beautiful.

Similar to how the vampire displayed an elegance in its movements while roaming the castle, so too did this bear an elegance when it occurred, for the ocean was *its* domain, and this was *its* mastery of roaming.

For when the monster was only three feet away from me, a colossal shark erupted into the air, taking with it the vampire between its primal jaws, then, arching gracefully mid air, fell back into the water nose first— creating only two splashes in its predatory dance of leaping out of the ocean to grab hold of its prey, rolling while suspended in the air so that the moonlight could reflect and reveal the different shades of silver upon its body, then crashing back into the body of water like a performer returning behind the curtains after their majestic debut.

I was left there awkwardly, like a petty creature misplaced in this world's madness after what had just ensued before my eyes, while beads of water gently rained down on my face from that last splash of the shark's departure.

And that awkwardness remained as I once again swam defeatedly towards the nearest shore I could see attached to the cliff's eventual end, and it never left me until I finally pulled myself out of the water and onto land, where I then sat outside of the tide's reach.

I watched over the rippling ocean as I collected my thoughts, regained proper motor control of my body, and dissipated the fight or flight state of being I had been held hostage by for so long.

I replayed so many moments in my head over and over again, though they lacked the emotions which previously accompanied them for I was now utterly drained.

I kept questioning and trying to make sense of so many things— especially that large shark that appeared at the very end and saved my life.

My guess, or rather, the rationalizing and justifying I came up with as to why I was still alive despite everything— for most of it honestly did not make sense to me —was that the very odor that repelled me from the vampire while I was trapped in the castle with it, was the same exact thing which drew the shark to it.

For there was no other reason why the shark ate the beast and not me. No other reason as to why it didn't come back to consume me as well after, during my pathetic and long swim to the shore.

It must have been the scent— something that was repulsive to the occupants of land, which turned out to be alluring to the critters of sea.

And that was all I was left with to accept while pondering over these recent events which plagued my life, and all of its unforgiving chaotic aspects.

But regardless, this terrible chapter had finally closed, and whatever life had in store for me next could finally play out.

The wind continued blowing in a gentle breeze which dried up my wet body in the cold night. The ocean continued to push and pull in its never ending motion and exchange of momentum. And the moon continued its slow descent in preparation for the sun's turn to rise again.

And within it all, there I was, continuing my own part in these cycled movements of the world— leaving a dark tragedy of my life behind to embark on the next part of it, something that would surely be filled with more light and goodness as I would see to it that it did.

This horror was not to be thrown aside with waste. It shall serve me. An expanse to my understanding of both the world and myself. A guidance, as silly as that sounds, away from this spectrum of the universe that is riddled in madness and chaos.

In hope and tranquility I'll stand, for I have tasted the nectar of blooms that grow in this darker region of existence, and find its ambrosia far too bitter of an application for that which I seek in this existential journey of discovery.

... But I must confess disappointedly... that nonetheless... I am lost.

I thought breaking free of that castle and successfully escaping my pursuer would come with a greater understanding of things, the world, the circumstances of life, or even myself.

But that is not the case.

I gained freedom... but no answers.

I achieved safety... but no further comfort.

I acquired relief... but no direction as to where to go now.

I wonder if this sensation of being lost is actually the success that comes with breaking free out of anything that once kept us trapped in whatever manner that may have been.

If we all thought that a knowing would immediately follow, or that answers would be attained during the process, or that a knowledge would've been collected along the way or at its end... when in fact, all of that merely became something now accessible since freedom has been achieved.

They were never something directly attached to the act of breaking free, but rather, they were things that could never be within the prisoner's reach or even an option of pursuit unless they broke free first.

But this is all just a ramble, and my adrenaline is finally letting up, and I can feel the peace from my mind slowing down.

It's a nice sensation, and I think I'm just going to enjoy it for a bit.

I've earned it.

END